Different Dogs

written by Pam Holden

1

This is a big dog.
It can help people
in the snow.

Saint Bernard

This is a little dog.
It is as little as a cat!

Chihuahua

What has this dog got?
It has ears that are
very long.

Basset Hound

What has this big dog got?
It has spots all over it.

Dalmatian

What has this little dog got?
It has hair that is very long.

Pomeranian

This big dog has long legs.
It can run very fast in
a race.

Greyhound

This little dog has short legs. Its tail is very short, too.

Yorkshire Terrier

German Shepherd

This dog is very big.
It can swim fast.